STAGED FRIGHT

A John Martin Story

by

James Warren McAllister

Cover Design and Art Work

By

James W. McAllister

This book is dedicated to all who have touched my life and passed on too soon.

Table Of Contents

Prologue

My name is John Martin. I'm a detective in the NYPD. It's not a bad job, really, as long as you don't mind long hours, low pay, no chance for a private life, and several people trying to kill you every day.

I became a cop so I could save the world, or so I thought. Investigating crimes seemed a way to make a real difference.

My partner and I were good at it. Real good.

Until he tried to kill me.

When I'd recovered, I had a new partner.

The perfect partner. That's what Mac said. Mac's my boss, Deputy Inspector Alice MacDonald.

Perfect. Sure.

Right.

So perfect, she cost me my wife.

Not that it was her fault.

It wasn't.

Strange things seem to happen around me lately. I can't explain why they happen, or how they seem to find me, but they're real. This is the story of one of those strange things. Several strange, fantastic, and surreal things actually.

I'm recording this because I hate typing. Besides, there's nothing to type on in this shoebox of an apartment. Mac told me to do what the NYPD's shrink said, and the shrink told me to stay home for three weeks and write this down.

Therapeutic.

Right.

If he likes it, I get to go back to work.

So I'm in my private little hellhole trying to record this. But there's a problem.

I'm out of Scotch.

Damn!

Unless there's some under these pizza boxes…

Well, whaddya know, a half bottle! It'll get me started on this thing at least.

I'd better start at the beginning.

I'll never forget that case.

For a lot of reasons.

But mostly because it cost me everything I loved…

1

I brushed the hair out of Lisa's eyes. I
could stare into those eyes forever. Her
jasmine smell filled me up to the
smiling point. My hands slid down her
bare shoulders, her hands sliding up my
chest and surrounding my neck. *I'm one
lucky SOB*, I thought as Doctor Lisa
Martin pulled my head down to her lips.
I could feel her heat pressing into my
chest as my wife's lips met mine.

Lisa elbowed me awake.

"John, the phone's ringing."

Dream shattered.

Did I mention that I hate telephones?

Lisa picked up the phone. She said
"yeah" a lot.

"Who is it?"

"Be right there." She hung up the
phone and walked to the closet, "I've
been called to a crime scene, John. See
you tonight, I hope. Or maybe sooner,
since you're on call." Lisa's lips
brushed my forehead and her smell faded

until I heard the door close. I opened my eyes and glanced at the clock.

"But, she just got here…" The life of a NYPD detective is tough enough. When his wife is the Medical Examiner, well…

"Just me and my dream. Again."

Just me and the ringing phone.

I rolled over and grabbed it, trying to gauge if we could afford a broken window. We couldn't.

Damn.

"Martin."

"Get your lazy ass out of bed!" Napoleon Holloway's voice always made him seem bigger than he was.

Po is six-feet eleven inches tall. When he slouches. He wears a dark grey fedora. Everywhere. I have no idea how much he weighs. A little less than Mount Rushmore I think.

Just more chiseled.

"Po, it's 3-friggin'-A.M. Our shift doesn't start for…"

"We're on call this week, remember?"

Damn.

"It's bad enough when you don't get to sleep with your wife, but when they don't even let you dream about it…"

"John, c'mon, man."

"Yeah, okay… Where?" I stood up and stretched. That felt good.

"Pick up some coffee, the usual, on your way in." Po only drank coffee from this little shop near my place. 16 ounces, one sugar, no cream, "Meet me at the precinct in 30. And, John?"

"Yeah?"

"Don't eat anything spicy."

Damn!

I love my old Crown Vic. Except when I'm trying to park it at the precinct. Or anywhere else in Manhattan. Or Brooklyn. Or the rest of New York City. This city never sleeps because everyone's looking for a parking spot.

I nudged into the only spot left in the precinct parking garage. Green lettering said something about 'environmentally friendly vehicles only'.

Right.

Let 'em arrest me.

I fit the car in okay. Now I just had to get out of it.

Did I mention that I'm a big guy? Not Napoleon Holloway big. I'm 'just' six feet five inches tall and around 235.

Okay, maybe closer to 240.

I had managed to squeeze out of the Crown Vic's passenger door before I remembered the coffees.

Damn.

It's a good thing Lisa keeps me limber. Well, when we are both home at the same time, anyway.

Which is like, never.

After another round of 3D Twister, I stood looking at my car. The good news was the 'environmentally friendly vehicles only' stencil was completely covered. The bad news was I'd forgotten to lock the doors.

Well, unless the precinct's parking garage was inhabited by dwarf car thieves, I figured it was okay. I hit the elevator button.

"You're late, partner!" Even at a whisper Po's voice shook the pictures on the wall. He grabbed the coffee with a

hand the size of Rhode Island. A hand
the size of Vermont pushed me back into
the elevator.

"Is Mac in yet?"

"Not yet. We need to go. You drive."
He hit the button and the doors closed.

Po always wanted me to drive. My car
doesn't cramp him as much as most. He
downed half the coffee in one gulp.

"Where?"

"Harlem. I've got the address here…"

New York City traffic is nowhere near
as bad as people think. At least before
4 A.M. anyway.

You can always spot an early morning
crime scene. An island of noise, lights,
and activity in a sea of dark yellow
rippled with shadows. It's never really
completely dark in The City.

And it was raining. It always rains
when we're on call. I think Mac uses the
Farmer's Almanac to schedule us.

I liked arriving at crime scenes with
Po. Everyone just…parted. I always
walked one step behind and to the right
of him. That was his idea, and since he
has six months' seniority on me, I

didn't argue. Ok, I didn't argue because he's bigger than me, too. But mostly it was the seniority.

"Holloway, Martin! This way." A uniformed cop called us from the stoop of a brownstone. He held onto the railing a little too tight. And he looked way too pale.

"You all right, Kawalski?"

"I think so, Lieutenant Martin. The scene's up here. It's prett…" Kawalski was still a rookie, only about three months on the job. He'll be a good cop, if seeing this crap every day doesn't drive him off the force.

Po rested one of those huge hands on the rookie's shoulder, "You'll be fine. Just remember, this is the crap we're here to stop."

Kawalski just shook his head and swallowed hard, "Follow me, detectives," he opened the door and stepped into the building. "The family is in my squad car. They're pretty shook up."

"You didn't show them this…"

"They were tied up in here."

The door didn't open to hallways and apartments; the door opened to the smell of blood so strong you could taste it. Inside was one big room, a dozen tables with two chairs each. A bar ran along the far wall. Opposite the bar was a stage. Three chairs were close to the stage, facing it. Ropes hung off of them.

In the middle of the stage was…

It took my brain ten seconds to figure out that I was looking at the victim.

Most of her.

Well, some of her.

A naked woman's torso was strapped into the blood soaked chair. On the stage around her were her…

I turned away.

The smell followed me, not letting me push that image from my mind.

I felt a huge hand on my back.

"Good God!" Po had turned away too. His eyes were closed, his head moving side to side slowly.

I turned around and forced myself to look at the crime scene as a professional detective. I couldn't look at it as a person.

Two fingers had rolled or fallen or were thrown from the stage to the main floor. Four were scattered around the victim's chair. Four were…not here.

Her arms had been…

I had to turn away again. I made a mental note to buy Kawalski a Scotch. Soon.

Her arms had been cut at the joints. Hands severed at her wrists, arms at her elbows, and her shoulders. Her legs had gotten the same attention, feet severed at the ankle, legs severed at the knees and hips.

The smell was just overpowering.

It drove me back without me knowing it. Until my back hit the wall.

I put my hands out to my sides and closed my eyes…

He had a black turtleneck and black jeans on. Black sneakers. Black socks. He wore a black ski mask that didn't hide his sadistic grin. He held a big knife, the serrated edge shining under the stage lights.

She was tied to the chair, hands tied to her thighs. No gag. She was sobbing, a tired sob, like she'd screamed and cried herself out.

She was young, dark, and pretty. Her eyes were red, her face flushed. Terrified.

She stared at the thing in black. It pranced around her, skipping like a little kid, laughing, taunting…

There was an audience. A man about forty and two women, one in her early teens and one the same age as the man. All three were tied to chairs, facing the stage.

Forced to watch.

The thing in black made a theatrical sweep with the knife. Blood spurted from her hand as the girl's left pinky hit the floor.

She was screaming now. Trying to move. Panicked. Terrified. Agonized.

This time the thing in black stopped next to her right hand. It bowed to the audience, picked up her right hand, and took his time sawing through the bone of her right pinky. As the severed finger *fell, the monster pointed the girl's hand at the audience. The blood covered the girl's family.*

The girl's toes went next. Little to big. Then the rest of her fingers.

As the thing started sawing her left ankle, the scene got foggy. The girl had passed out by the time he finished. I think she was dead when her arms were cut off. I could barely see her now through the mist. Dark, smoky almost. I felt… something coming. Big. Dark. Irresistible.

Evil.

I couldn't run. It was almost on me. I couldn't see it, but I could feel its mouth open, I could smell the decayed breath. It smelled of death…

"JOHN!"

Lisa, somewhere far off, far away.

"JOHN MARTIN!"

Po's voice shook the windows. Lisa shook me.

"John, what happened? Are you all right?"

"I need to si…"

The vomit cut me short.

The room spun around and everyone went out of focus.

"He's going into shock. Lay him down here." Lisa's voice seemed way too stressed. All I needed was an hour of sleep.

The crack of her hand on my cheek ended that thought.

"Ow! Oh, man…"

"Drink this. Little sips. Better?"

"That was Po's coffee! Needs sugar. Damn." How do I tell them, tell her what happened?

I didn't even know myself.

"I saw it."

Having the medical examiner and half a dozen NYPD officers and detectives stare at you like you have three heads isn't good for your psyche.

"You saw what?" At least Po didn't rattle the windows this time.

"The murder. More like torture." I sucked in half the air in the room. "Black turtleneck, black jeans, black sneakers, black ski mask. Big, serrated knife. The perp danced around like a mad jester or something. Taunting the girl, the audience. One sick bastard."

"John, what are you saying? You saw the crime?" Lisa looked, well, skeptical is a kind enough description.

"I don't know how. It was like I was there. Watching. He's 5' 10", about 175. Couldn't see any hair, didn't hear him say anything. His teeth are yellow."

"John Martin, first you ruin my coffee, then you contaminate the crime scene, now you're telling me…"

"Yeah. That's what happened."

"Let's suppose, just suppose now, that what you're saying is true. Why did this guy do this?"

"Evil. Just plain evil."

Lisa finished wiping my face. At least I didn't puke all over her.

I glanced at my pants.

Damn.

Fortunately, I keep a change of clothes in the Crown Vic. Lisa brought the pants to me.

"He'll do it again," I warned as I dropped my drawers.

"Yeah. I was afraid you'd say that."

"Holloway, look, here." Kawalski was pointing to the bloody stage.

Footprints.

Sneakers.

I stepped into the clean trousers and walked to Po while I zipped.

"Let's follow the trail," Po slapped my back.

The footprints led into a storeroom. They faded out about five feet before a door.

"It's gotta go into the alley."

"So open it already."

Po looked at me.

"Did you really see it?"

"Yeah. I'm like," I took a big breath and swallowed a subway car, "trying to forget it, ya know?"

"Don't blame ya." Po grabbed the doorknob. "I'd have puked too."

"Thanks for the support."

"It's what partners do."

The alley smelled like everything tossed out of every restaurant in Manhattan had ended up here.

About a week ago.

The cold drizzle didn't help the smell at all.

We went over the alley twice. Nothing. As we walked out to the street, I slipped and reached a hand out for the wall.

The thing in black jogged toward the street. It stopped, ripped the ski mask off and tossed it into the dumpster before heading onto the street.

"John?"

Did I mention that Po's face is really big?

"Ski mask is in the dumpster. It went left on the street. Medium brown hair, medium length. Didn't see the face."

"Cleo's working in town this weekend." Po's little sister, nationally known as Cleopatra. A dozen platinum records. Angelic voice and a great kid. Po's really proud of her. "She's playing at the Excelsior Club Saturday night. I'll get tickets if you and Lisa…" Po grabbed the mask with his forceps and stuffed it into a zip-lock bag.

"Yes! Po, you know we love her voice. When's she getting into town?"

"Tuesday afternoon."

"You two come for dinner Friday then. Lisa'll make her Mac & Cheese."

"I can't resist that." Po just stared at me. "John?"

"Yeah?"

"Is this shit real?"

"Seeing what happened?"

"Yeah."

"I wish it wasn't."

"I hear that partner. I don't envy seeing that shit. I don't think I could handle watching what this guy does."

"I don't know if it's a guy or not."

"Friday night. Eight okay?"

"Perfect."

We'd come to the Crown Vic. Lisa stood there staring at us.

"So, you were gonna tell us when?"

I've been partnered with Po for more than three years. I've only seen two people make him cower. His little sister could, got it from their mom Po says. Lisa is the other one.

"Friday night you're making Mac & Cheese. Saturday we're going to the

Excelsior Club." Hey, I've got my partner's back.

"Yeah Doc. What John done said."

"Stop that talk, Napoleon Holloway," she looked mad until Po grinned at her, "you big lug!"

Did I mention that I love my wife?

"Only one catch. We need to have this case solved by noon Tuesday…"

2

"Holloway! Martin! Get your sorry asses in here!"

I looked at Po.

He looked at me.

"One, two, three…"

I threw scissors.

Po threw a rock.

Damn.

"John, you always throw scissors!" Po shook his head.

"C'mon, rockhead." Po followed me into Mac's office.

"Well?" Mac has a unique voice when she's gotten heat from upstairs. The effect is sort of like chalk grating on your eyeballs.

From the inside.

"We've got DNA from the ski mask. No matches. Williams and Reichert interviewed the victim's family. They have no idea who it could be; there's no debt, business partners, rivals, nothing on those angles." I took a big breath. Mac didn't look any happier.

"The victim's name was Stella Hanratty," I began. "NYU Junior. Polly-Sci major. Williams and Reichert interviewed a dozen of her classmates. Nothing there. All indications are that everyone liked the kid."

I let out a big breath.

And I waited.

Mac always let loose at the one talking.

That was always me.

I never remembered Po knew about the scissors.

"You two think you're the best damned detectives in New York. Hell, the entire East Coast! Martin, you wonder why I've kept you in the middle of the promotion list? And Holloway, you keep wondering why I won't give you a recommendation for the FBI? Here's a reason: two days into this, and all the two of you've got is a ski mask that Martin *thinks* the perp wore?

"THAT'S ALL?"

"Any suggestions, Boss?" Po's 'soft' voice never worked on Mac, but he still tried it. He's a good partner.

"You're missing something. This doesn't look like revenge, jealousy, or greed. It's not a 'one-hit-wonder' M.O."

I could see the veins bulge on Mac's red face.

"You think this is a psycho of some kind?"

I really wish I could learn to think before I talk. Guess I'm just not wired that way.

"Duh-UH! Now go get me SOMETHING USEFUL!"

Mac raised her arm, boney finger pointing to the door.

I'm not sure how I beat Po out of Mac's office.

I'm not sure how we ended up at the crime scene.

"Hold on a minute. Wait until Lisa gets here."

"Why?"

"Because you scared the Bejesus out of me the last time. Having a doc around while you 'see' makes sense."

Po's logic was usually flawless.

"Why here, do you think?"

"Well," Po rubbed his chin, "He wanted an audience. We know she was in here, and left just before the club closed. Likely, he grabbed her as she came out of the place, held her somewhere until everyone left. The family says she called them and asked them to come here. All she would say is it was an emergency.

"And he wanted to be on stage."

"Why the audience?"

"I'd guess he needs them."

"Yeah. He was dancing around here," I pointed to the stage, "like he was performing."

"John! Po!"

Lisa's voice always makes me smile.

"Hello, Doc." Po made a show of removing his hat and bowing.

I think it's why he wears the fedora.

"John, are you sure this is a good idea?" She stood up on her tiptoes and kissed my cheek.

I smiled.

"I dunno. We've got nothing else, and Mac thinks this guy'll do it again. I do too."

She took a big breath and tried to force a smile.

It almost worked.

God, I love her.

"Just be careful." She set her bag on a table near the stage and opened it.

"How do I do that? I don't even know what this is."

"Just, if you can, don't take chances," Po looked down at me from under his grey fedora, "I don't have the temperament to break in a new partner."

"Yeah, right."

"Well, let's get going. Start 'seeing' or whatever."

"I don't know how!"

"What were you doing last time?"

"Let's see. I backed away from the stage until my back was against this wall," I took the same position.

Nothing.

"Wait, you had your eyes closed, and your hands spread out against the wall."

I took the position Po remembered.

It was like a movie, starting where it'd left off.

The thing in black hacked at the girl's right shoulder. She'd found her peace well before. The audience had passed out.

The monster stomped his foot once, screamed at the audience, but they didn't wake up. There's only so much one can take…

He seemed deflated now. He finished cutting the arm off, but his enjoyment was gone.

I watched him pick up four fingers and stuff them in his pocket. He took two steps toward the back of the stage.

The thing in black stopped.

It turned around.

It stared. Right at me.

Then it turned to my right. Where Po was.

It smiled. A wicked, evil smile.

The monster turned and left the stage. The vision started to fade, then cleared and sharpened again.

Some kind of mist came in, dark and dank.

Behind it came…something.

It was a long way away.

22

It was big.

Huge.

And it was coming fast.

Very fast.

For me.

"John. Look at me, John." Lisa patted my cheek twice before she slapped it.

Hard.

"OW!"

"You okay partner?"

I looked at Lisa, then Po.

Then Lisa.

She's a lot prettier than Po.

"Yeah. Something… I don't know. I've got to think about this."

"Let's take a break. We'll talk it over when you've had a chance to digest what you've seen."

"It's 6:30. Po, come on over for dinner. We'll talk about it after we eat."

"Sure thing, Doc!"

Traffic was light and we didn't have to cross any bridges or tunnels, so it only took us a half hour to drive the two miles to our place.

"You two go easy on the Scotch while I cook the hot dogs. You'll never solve this if you pass out, and there's no cash in the budget for another bottle this month. Mashed, fried, or rice?"

Po and I looked at each other.

We both knew Lisa was wrong.

We'd solved half our cases over a bottle of Scotch.

Po shrugged.

I poured.

"Rice is fine, Miss Lisa."

Po sat on the couch and reached up for the glass I offered him.

The couch groaned.

I thought of buying another one.

The price made me cringe.

"What do you think?" Po took a sip.

"He took four fingers with him. Then, Po…"

"What?"

"He stared at you. And smiled. More like a laugh, really. Like a lifer on parole staring in a cathouse window."

Po looked at my stained carpet for some time. He took another sip and looked me in the eye, head tilted.

24

His eyes narrowed some.

He looked…

Vicious.

"Let me get my hands on that bastard son of a…"

Did I mention that Po is black?

Really, really dark-skinned black.

His knuckles were turning white as he squeezed the whiskey glass.

"Po!"

He let out a big breath. He relaxed a little.

"It's just that, well…"

"Yeah. Me too."

Po and I were a lot alike.

We weren't doing this job for the multi-million dollar paychecks.

Or the fame and notoriety.

Or the convenient hours.

Or because Mac was a great person to work for.

We both hated things like this thing in black.

We'd solved almost every case we'd been assigned to.

And some we weren't assigned to.

"He gets off on the terror, the reactions of the audience more than that of the victim. She was gone before he was done. After the audience passed out, he looked deflated. From then on, it was like he was cutting up a hog. He looked bored."

"Maybe he's a butcher?"

"Some type of theatrical background?"

"How many butchers that were failed actors can there be in New York?"

"Not more than two thousand. Tops."

I poured another round.

Po leaned in close, "What are you getting her?" He nodded toward the kitchen.

"Getting her? What, it's not her birthday. What?"

A fist the size of a locomotive slammed my shoulder.

"Your anniversary is a week from tomorrow! Damn, John, that's one prime woman you've conned into marrying you. She's worth working to keep."

"Damn. Po, I've never been good at that stuff. Thanks."

"Do I have to remind you every day?"

"Are you two still conscious in there?" Lisa called from the kitchen.

I looked at Po and whispered, "Yes. Please!"

Then I yelled, "What? Huh? Wastimese izzit?"

"Not funny John!"

Po laughed.

Lisa brought out a tray of hotdogs and set them on the table next to the bowl of rice.

"Dinner!"

For such a big man, Po can move very fast.

"Mustard's here, brown sugar and nutmeg for the rice is there," Lisa motioned at the condiments on the counter.

"Thank you Lord for that of which we are about to partake!" Po always said grace.

A dozen hotdogs and a pound of rice later, Po said, "Doc, thank you for that wonderful feast!"

"It was nothing, really. Now, how about this psycho-bastard killer?" Lisa handed Po a glass of Scotch, then me, then she poured herself one.

"Someone who needs an audience. Who feeds off of the audience's emotions."

"But not good emotions. He's not up there with a feather." I took a sip of the whiskey.

"What would make some one need that? A failed acting career? Some type of trauma?"

"Acting maybe. If coupled with the trauma." Po sipped from his glass, "I'd think it'd be a big trauma though."

"Are you boys sure it's a 'he'?" Lisa gulped half of her glass, watching us over the rim.

I looked at Po.

He was looking at me.

That's when the phone rang.

"Dr. Martin."

Po and I watched Lisa's face change as she set her whiskey glass down. She looked at me and mouthed something.

I shrugged.

She rolled her eyes, "Corner of Peck's Slip and Water Street. Right.

Don't touch anything. I'm on my way."

She hung up and glared at me, "M. A. P."

"I thought you said 'Mac.'"

"Well, she'll be calling you next, so let's go."

The phone rang.

I reached for it, but Po picked it up, "Martin. Mac, can't talk. Running down a lead. Later."

Yeah, great partner.

"After I fed you and everything!" I grabbed my coat.

"What 'everything'? You're not my type. Besides, you're married," Po slid a huge arm into his jacket and grabbed his fedora.

"Hurry up boys, or I'm driving."

I pulled the Crown Vic off of Pearl Street onto Peck's Slip. A half dozen black & whites flashed red on the bricks outside of Acqua's restaurant.

Kawalski walked up as we got out.

"We found one of the missing fingers," he pointed underneath one of the sidewalk tables.

"Thanks. Anything else?"

"We've cased the area four blocks around. Nothing."

"Thanks, Kawalski," Po patted his back and almost toppled the guy.

The restaurant's owner was a middle aged man, died black hair, black suit, medium build. Pretty upset. Po nodded to me.

I flashed him my badge.

"I'm detective Martin. This is my partner, detective Holloway. What happened here?"

"The lady, she…we heard…the lady, she scream. Her date yell and jump up. He almost knock my waitress down," the man was wringing his hands, "At first, we think it's a fake, trying to get a free meal. But something tell me no, this is real. We didn't let no one touch it or nothing."

"Did you see anyone around dressed in black?"

"What? Yes, of course. My staff, they all wear black."

"Anyone else? Maybe acting suspicious-like?" I glanced at my

partner. Po had his pad out, talking to
a waitress a few feet away.

"People walk by all the time. Some
stop and look at the specials menu. Some
peak inside. I don't notice nothing
unusual."

"Okay. Thanks. Hang around in case we
need something."

"You hungry? I feed you and your
partner. No more customers tonight," he
gave a shrug.

I felt sorry for the guy. It looked
like a nice place. The menu looked good,
northern Italian.

"Thanks, we've eaten already." I felt
something, and glanced at Po.

He was glaring at me.

Seems he was still hungry.

Lisa grabbed my arm and leaned in
close.

Her smell.

Jasmine.

I forgot about the case.

Something had come up.

"I'll have to run tests, but it looks
like her right ring finger."

Damn.

Deflated again.

"I've got an idea," I looked around the area. A bunch of restaurants, a few small offices, a hotel around the corner on Pearl Street.

Po was standing next to me. He looked around too.

"You thinkin'…"

"Yeah. Let's get the statements from the diners and staff, then clear them out. I don't need an audience."

It took us about half an hour to wrap it up. No one saw anything unusual. The owner gave us the names of all the patrons who paid by credit card that night. Only two parties paid cash.

We had no clue about how long the finger could have been there.

Once the patrons and staff left, I motioned to Lisa and Po.

Then I backed up against the bricks of the building. I spread my arms out, took a deep breath, and closed my eyes.

Black jacket over a black turtleneck, black jeans, black sneakers. Shoulder length black hair. No blood stains.

The monster walked, head down. It stopped at the chalkboard menu, head moving back and forth as if reading…

It was a subtle movement, from chin to pocket to mouth. The flick was short and fast after its hand left the pocket.

The finger rolled under the vacant table.

The thing in black licked its fingers as it walked away at a leisurely pace. At the end of the block it crossed the street, and disappeared into the restaurant there.

"John. Hey, John."

The scene shrunk away as if it was sucked into a pinhole.

"We need a list of diners at Nelson's Blue restaurant."

Nelson's Blue sat kitty-corner, about a hundred yards from Acqua's.

Not exactly front row seats.

From the descriptions of the reactions at Acqua's, it was close enough.

"It watched. Gambled the finger wouldn't be found until it was seated by the window at Nelson's."

"Probably had a nice glass of wine and enjoyed the show," Po had that look on his face. Like, if he saw the thing in black now, they'd have to call Lisa instead of Kawalski.

"Chardonnay."

I looked at my wife.

Her face wore the same look as Po's.

I turned to look across the plaza.

"Actually, it was a red Zinfandel."

3

"They're right-a this way, Detectives. I watch-a the Law ana Order, so I-sa know about contaminating the evidence. I donna let no-one a-touch them. They're right-a over here…"

The fellow must have been the inspiration for the chef in The Lady and the Tramp. Po grunted a thank you while I snapped some pics.

After about a dozen pics, Lisa pushed past me. She grabbed them with forceps and dropped them into a Ziploc bag.

Two fingers.

"I'll run the DNA on these…"

"Yeah, good idea. Could be someone else's…"

"John! Be nice to that little lady!" Po's admonishment vibrated my vertebrae.

I looked at Lisa.

She looked at me.

Cold.

Icy.

Frigid!

DAMN!

Then she smiled.

Birds sang. I swear!

We both laughed.

Lisa went off to do her laboratory thing. Po just shook his head.

"You need to be careful, my friend. She's special, a real keeper. You could at least work on keeping her happy a little bit…"

"Yeah. Damn, Po, you're right." I sank into the chair…

It came into the restaurant, all in black. Except for the mask. But I couldn't see the face.

It ordered a red Zinfandel and Carpaccio. Sipped wine. Licked the raw beef before eating it…

Paid the bill in cash. Left a good tip, and the two fingers

Then it turned to face me. It smiled, its face…

CRACK!

Stars. Pain. More stars.

"John!"

"Damn! Po, what was that for? Damn!"

"You were off in a trance somewhere. It spooks me when you do that."

"Next time, try NOT to break my jaw, okay?"

"Sorry."

"I almost had the face! Damn!"

"Look, we've interviewed everyone here, Lisa's off for half the night doin' her DNA thing. What's say you come back to my place. Cleo'll be there by now. She'd love to see you."

"Well, I guess it's okay."

As long as Lisa didn't know.

You wouldn't like her when she's jealous.

We took off for Po's place, up in Harlem. We stopped by the Dinosaur BBQ and grabbed some pulled pork, chili and salt potatoes for Cleo. I carried the food while Po unlocked the door.

After fumbling for about an hour, he pulled the door open.

"Sweaty!" Cleo jumped up to give Po a kiss.

"Heh," I laughed, "don't you mean 'sweetie'?"

"You didn't grow up with him!"

Did I mention that Po was a bit taller than me?

37

Cleo's sweater flew up as she wrapped her arms around Po's neck.

Damn!

"Heh-he-heh…" Po's laugh filled the hallway.

"Oh! Po, who…" Cleo slid down until her feet hit the ground.

Damn!

"John Martin!" She squealed and planted a kiss on my neck.

"Eh, Cleo, nice to…see you!"

"C'mon kids, let's get in and eat. I'm starved."

Dinner was good. Po and Cleo gabbed.

I wished Lisa was there.

"Hey, Po, where's the ice cream?" Cleo loved ice cream.

And Po loved his little sister.

'Oh, crap. I'll run out and get some."

I'd never seen him move so fast.

"So, Johnny…"

Somehow Cleo was on the couch, next to me.

About as next to me as she could get.

Damn!

"What's married life like?"

A finger hit my chin and started down...

"Um, well, it's, eh..."

Lips hit my cheek.

"You're too easy!" Cleo laughed and stood up.

Then she stretched.

Both arms up high, onto her tiptoes...

Damn!

"Cleo, do, I don't, um..."

"Relax Johnny! I'm just teasin' ya!"

She turned away from me and winked at me over her shoulder.

"I know you're a good boy."

She turned around, bent down, and kissed my forehead.

Did I mention that her sweater was a loose fitting V neck?

A deep V neck.

Damn.

I took a deep breath, "Cleo, you're killin' me here!"

She was in my lap.

Her lips pressed to mine.

She tasted like strawberries.

Her tongue pressing in...

DAMN!

I opened for her.

Hey, I'm human.

I think.

I pushed her back.

"Cleo! I can't." I lifted her by her hips and set her on her feet as I stood up.

"I'd better go."

She giggled, "Why, did something come…"

"Cleo! Stop it. Tell Po I'll see him in the morning."

I drove home with the windows open.

I poured a Scotch and sat down. The first sip tasted like strawberries…

DAMN!

I prefer jasmine.

I put the Scotch down and headed for the bathroom.

I didn't make it.

"John, I'm home!"

For some reason I turned around.

Bad move.

"John, the DN…" Lisa's mouth just stopped moving, hanging open like an empty restroom stall.

"Uh…"

Brilliant.

Damn!

I stood there, Cleo's strawberry lipstick smeared on my face and neck.

I tried a smile.

Bad move.

It was on my teeth too.

"Lisa, Cleo, I, um… It wasn't like with you…"

Damn!

"Arrgh!"

Lisa turned and left.

Strawberry lipstick and Scotch isn't too bad.

I think.

I don't remember the last half of the bottle.

I do remember Po pounding on my door.

Until it opened.

Okay, he hit it once.

"John, get up! What's your problem?"

"Illbeoutimamin."

"Oh, crap!"

I blinked a few times. I tried to sit up.

Bad idea.

I smelled coffee.

"Porgetmeacuspleses."

"Damn fine time he picks to piss off Lisa and go on a jag. I oughtta…"

Po's mumbles are like most people's yells.

Through a bullhorn.

"Geesh, Po. Not so damn loud!"

"You shut your mouth and drink this. I need a partner today, not a drunken sailor recovering from shore leave."

"Thanks." I drank.

After about four cups I felt almost human.

"Po, it's three A-friggin-M!"

"Yeah. Cleo told me what happened. You should have cleaned up her lipstick before Lisa saw it. I asked Cleo to call her, to set things straight."

"Bad idea."

"What do you mean?"

"Lisa won't hear what she says. She'll hear 'he's mine now.' Trust me."

"Aw, John, Lisa's not like that…"

"The hell she's not. I don't help it any. I try to explain, but I just make things worse."

"Look, let the girls handle this for now. We need to go. Now."

"Another one?"

"Yeah. That old theater off Broadway, The Cameo. Not good. Six on stage. Each made to watch the others. The last one…"

"Damn."

"Someone noticed the blood running out under the doors."

"What? I've been to that theater as a kid. The stage is a good long way from the doors."

"I know. The blood under the doors was a plant, a way to get some one inside to see the real show."

"Okay. Let's go. But, Po?"

"Yeah?"

"You drive."

"Good idea."

The place was worse than I expected. The blood and gore and the Scotch and pizza conspired against me.

I lost.

No one noticed.

Or, at least they didn't let on if they had.

Hell, even Po blew lunch.

Or was it breakfast?

Once I'd cleaned up, Po was waiting for me.

"John, can you…"

"Oh, no. No, no, no! No!"

"John, there's nothing else. We need to find this guy and stop him."

Damn.

"Bring a bucket."

I climbed the three steps onto the stage, walked to the middle of it, and closed my eyes.

They were all asleep. Or unconscious. I couldn't tell.

Not that it mattered.

It moved around them, weaving in and out.

Like a shark.

Buckets next to each chair.

When all six were awake, the thing in black removed the gags.

Then it played 'eenie, meenie, miny, mo…'.

The youngest one lost.

Her chair was dragged out in front, so she'd have to watch what happened to the others.

Then it started.

The father yelled.

He screamed when the first finger hit the floor.

He struggled, almost knocking his chair over with the second.

The father was panting hard. The youngest girl was crying loudly.

The thing in black cut off another finger.

And another.

Everyone was screaming, pleading, swearing, threatening.

Everyone except the youngest.

She just cried as the thing cut up her father.

He drained the blood into the buckets.

When it stopped dripping, he moved to the oldest son.

He didn't scream.

Until the fourth finger.

His younger sister was next.

She'd started praying when dad stopped moving.

The thing in black put the knife to her left pinkie.

She passed out.

So the thing moved to Grandma.

The old lady just glared at him.

Even after her blood stopped dripping into the bucket.

The older sister was next.

Then it was the mom and the youngest.

It asked mom to choose which died first.

She just screamed, eyes wild.

It played eenie, meenie again.

The little girl's sobs shook the chair.

The thing walked to the mom…

It's not a smooth ride in the back of an ambulance racing down Broadway.

At least I think that's where we were.

Everything flashed in and out.

What I saw between the ambulance and the hospital…

Dark, evil things. Things without shape, without names…

All looking for, coming for me.

I really couldn't tell you what they were.

But claws were reaching for me, almost…

Something touched my cheek.

"GODDAMMIT JOHN!"

Lisa can be very loud at times.

Thank God.

The lights in the Emergency Room washed the darkness away.

My cheek began to hurt.

Lisa's got a good left hook.

"John, John…"

I could look into those eyes forever.

"Lisa, I… I'm sorry about Cleo…"

Did I mention that Lisa has a great right cross?

I watched her storm out of the room. Po turned his head to watch her. Then he looked at me.

"You'll never learn to keep your mouth shut, will you." He just shook his head slowly, "You all right? I thought you'd died back there."

"Yeah, me too. This thing. It's… Evil. Po, it's pure capital "E" Evil. It cut them up for the effect on the others, but mostly to drain their blood.

Then it poured buckets full into the street."

"Where'd he go?"

"I'm not sure it's a 'he', Po. I don't know where it went, something ca… it came…"

I heard some type of alarm go off, and a lot of people screaming things like 'code' and 'arrest' and 'crash cart.'

When I woke up, everything hurt. Especially my chest.

Lisa was holding my hand.

"Damn!"

"Shut up."

I shut up.

I know when I'm licked.

Well, sometimes anyway.

Lisa caressed my soul.

Some time later I was staring at Po as he walked into the room. Lisa was asleep, still holding my hand.

She was going to have a stiff neck when she woke up.

"John, are you okay?"

Cleo's voice slinked around Po.

Lisa sat up.

Damn!

Cleo stepped out from behind Po, "Lisa, I, I'm so sorry."

Lisa glared back through steaming silence.

"I was wrong. Please, forgive me."

Lisa made a noise.

I can't describe it.

"Lisa, I've had a talk with Cleo. It won't happen again."

Po's deep voice is very powerful when it's quiet. It worked very well on Lisa.

Almost too well…

"Okay."

Damn!

"Lisa, it was me, not John…."

"I said 'OK'. Drop it."

Lisa's words fell on Cleo like an avalanche.

Fast.

Cold.

Final.

Followed by silence.

"John's going to be all right. It seems something happens when he…"

"I need someone to help me back."

"That's my job." That glare was aimed at Po this time.

"Now, Lisa, this is new to all of us…"

"I know. Just remember. Don't let him unless I'm there. Ever."

"Hey, don't I get a say in thi…"

"No!" three voices chorused.

Damn.

It's nice to know people care that much about you.

But it's a bitch to give up that much control.

4

They wouldn't let me go back to work for three days.

Nothing happened on the case for those days.

Not that Po wasn't working. There just weren't any leads for him to follow.

The first morning back I walked into the precinct.

"Martin! My office. NOW!" Mac shot the words at me.

I took a deep breath and followed her.

"Close the damned door."

Great.

"Martin," she softened her voice a bit, "John, what the hell is Po talking about?"

Gee, Mac, like, give me a clue?

"About what?"

"You 'see' crimes? WHAT THE HELL IS THAT!"

It's hard to swallow Long Island.

"Well, Mac…."

"Well WHAT?"

"I can see what happened. But…"

"WHAT THE HELL DO YOU MEAN?"

I stared at Mac.

When she got like this, it was my only defense.

After about an hour she said, "Tell me."

So I did.

"I should send you for a Psych Eval."

Damn.

If you want to strike terror in the heart of any NYPD detective, just say the words 'Psych Eval.'

Never fails.

"Mac, I…"

Her phone rang.

I waited.

She said 'yeah' a lot.

Then she said 'and' a lot.

She said "SHIT!" just before she slammed the phone down.

Damn!

"There's been another one. Go with Po. Solve the damn case!"

I got out of Mac's office.

Fast.

"John! We're meeting Lisa at the scene. Get a move on."

Yeah. Nice to see you back, partner!

"Nice to be back."

"What?"

"Never mind."

"Anyway, I'm glad you're back."

We pulled up to the New York Grain Terminal. The huge crumbling warehouse once stored grain brought from Indiana and Ohio across the Great Lakes and down the Erie Canal. The terminal loaded ships that took the grain all over the world.

Now it sat unused, a rotting hulk of a building on Brooklyn's waterfront.

I parked next to Lisa's M.E. van. She was leaning against it, waiting.

"This way. I made sure no one touched anything. Watch your step…" Lisa took a giant step over an ugly puddle, "I made sure the curious uniforms barfed well away from the crime scene."

Great.

"This… this doesn't fit. This is an empty warehouse. No stage. Any audience?"

"No. But there's something else," Lisa stopped next to the body.

What was left of it.

It just lay there in the middle of the huge warehouse, the headless torso of some poor guy, a grotesque island in an ocean of blood.

Off to the right, across the open space of the warehouse, something caught my eye.

I started walking.

"John?" I heard Lisa's sensible heels and Po's monster Oxfords following.

About halfway to it I stopped. I knew what it was before I could see what it was.

It was a leg.

When I got to it, I opened the door and looked around. At the far end of the parking lot was the other one.

I ran.

It took me a little longer this time, but I spotted it a few hundred yards off.

Well, the seagulls gave it away.

An arm.

It took Lisa and Po a few minutes to catch up.

"John," Po rested his hands on his knees, "what the hell?"

"Crumbs."

"What?"

"It's a trail of crumbs. For us to follow..." I scanned around.

Nothing.

"John, maybe we should..."

I let out a big breath. "Yeah."

We walked back to the body. I backed up against the closest wall and closed my eyes.

It was dressed the same. All black. The sleeves and legs glistened in the scattered light in the warehouse.

It came in the far door, the one we'd gone out to find the arm. It dropped something near the door, then walked carefully toward the body. Two-thirds of the way it stopped and clapped, jumping up and down like a kid at Christmas.

The thing in black froze. It looked straight at me. It smiled. White teeth, too-red lips. It motioned with its arm.

"C'mon Johnny!"

The warehouse got darker after it spoke. The walls got closer.

It ran out the far door.

It was almost pitch black. The walls were just a few inches away.

I ran after it.

I got to the door, pulled it open and rushed through.

Without looking.

I ran into…

"JOHN!"

WHAAACK!

I heard the slap about two seconds before I felt it.

I was glad I could feel the sting.

"John? It's all right, John. You're here, you're back." Lisa looked worried.

"Why did Po hit me?"

"Hey, partner, that wasn't me! Look at your wife! Heh-heh."

"What was it, John?"

"John, what happened? You…you stopped breathing."

Damn!

How do you tell your wife you've stared into the face of…

"We need to go. Po, how far from the body to the leg?"

Po looked across the warehouse, "About twenty yards."

"And about fifty to the second leg. A hundred to the arm."

"So the other arm will be a two hundred…"

"In the same direction. Then a foot, about a quarter mile past the arm. A half mile past that, the other foot…"

"Then a hand, a mile out. Two miles past that, the other hand. Then the head, four miles out."

"Crumbs."

"Hansel and Gretel."

"Yeah, some fairytale. Do we know who the victim is?"

"Nothing here to go by. No ID, no wallet. A male, best guess is between 35 and 50. No prints until we find the hands. No dental until we find the head. I'll get some samples for DNA, so at least we can match up the…parts. And…"

"And?"

Lisa pointed to the floor.

"Damn!" Po gasped

J, O, H, N. In blood.

Great.

Po and I left to go looking for crumbs. When I put the key in the Crown Vic Po grabbed my hand.

"What was it? What did you see?"

I looked into those huge brown eyes.

I shook my head.

"Nothing. Just, nothing. Like 'end-of-the-universe' nothing…"

Po shivered and let go of my hand.

I drove in the general direction the parts were set in.

Po kept looking at me.

"What?"

"Why is it after you?"

"How the hell am I supposed to know?"

Po turned to look out the windshield, "Next time, ask."

We found the second foot, almost a mile from the body. A mile past that, the right hand.

We never found the rest.

It found us.

Mac called us. She wasn't happy.

Not that I've ever seen Mac happy.

Somebody found a head in Harlem. Outside of an apartment building.

Po's apartment building.

Po slapped the light on the roof and dialed Cleo's cell.

I hit the siren and drove.

I'd like to say I made record time from Brooklyn to Harlem, but it's New York. The traffic is what it is.

Cleo never answered her cell.

I could feel it building up in Po. Like steam in a boiler with the outlet plugged.

So I made sure we got there before the pressure hit critical mass.

I made record time from Brooklyn to Harlem.

I flashed my badge as Po barreled through the lobby. I hit the elevator button. Po waited three second before flying up the stairs.

Now, Po's in great shape for a six eleven, three hundred and something pound NYPD detective. And he can move incredibly fast when he needs to.

But Po's apartment was on the twenty second floor.

I got to Po's door three seconds before he did. He was panting and drenched, but he had the door open before my hand hit the buzzer.

Po burst into the apartment, gun drawn, with me right behind.

"Aaaark!" Cleo screamed.

And dropped her towel.

DAMN!

She'd just come out of the shower.

Po turned in a flash. His chest blocked my view.

"Napoleon! What the hell is going on?" Cleo had the towel back.

"Uh…"

"It's work related," I tried to find a civilized way to tell her about the head. "There's, um, some evidence outside the building." I gulped as Po turned around.

"You just about scared me out of my skin! Argh!" Cleo shook her head and stomped into her room. The door slammed shut behind her.

Po took a big breath. The pressure left as he exhaled slowly.

"We should still check the apartment…"

"AAAAAHHHH!"

The door to Cleo's room burst open and she flew naked into Po's arms.

I ran into the room.

The top dresser drawer was open.

Cleo had some interesting unmentionables.

And right there on top of them was the hand.

I scanned the room. I checked under the bed, behind the curtains, in the closet.

"Po, it's clear in here. I'm calling Lisa. It's…"

"The last crumb."

Po's voice was a quiet growl that scared the hell out of me.

"Po's place," I glanced out the door. Po had his gun out, holding Cleo and scanning the room. "No, everyone's okay. But we've found the other parts…"

I moved into the living room, then headed for Po's room. When that was clear, I checked the bathroom, just in case.

"The place is clear."

Po relaxed a little and holstered his gun.

"It's okay, sis. Nobody's here."

"But… but somebody was here! While I was…" She fell sobbing into Po's arms.

"You okay?" I nodded at Po, "As soon as Lisa gets here, I'll check the security tapes."

Cleo sobbed for the twenty minutes it took Lisa to get there.

Po just looked for something to…

I couldn't decide if it was crush or rip.

I was just glad it wasn't focused at me.

Lisa went into the room and did her M.E. thing. She took the hand and Cleo's… things that were in the drawer.

And she took Cleo with her.

When I'd finished collecting the security tapes, I dusted the apartment for prints.

That's when Internal Affairs showed up.

Usually these are the last guys a NYPD detective wants to see. But here was a detective whose apartment was violated, so they came in as fresh eyes, not blind to the wallpaper pattern so to speak.

And they had the clearance to look at every case Po had any involvement with. If it was one of Po's collars, they'd find 'em.

Plus, they'd secure the apartment until the NYPD locksmith could get there.

"They weren't after me, John." Po said quietly.

"Cleo? Why?"

"Well, I don't know the answer to that question. But you could…"

"With IA here? They'd lock me in the loony bin!"

"John, she's my little sister…"

Damn.

I went into Cleo's room. I stood with my back against her door and spread my arms out, palms about waist high against the door…

It moved into the room quickly, dressed in a janitor's uniform, carrying a tool bag. Except for the black ski mask.

It opened the door to Po's room first, then quickly closed it. It paused outside the bathroom. I could hear the shower running, Cleo singing...

It laughed quietly and slid into her room. It opened the drawer, took out one of Cleo's lacy things. It brought the lingerie up to its face and inhaled deeply...

It looked at me and smiled.

"Why me?"

It just laughed before it threw the lingerie back into the drawer. Then it opened its bag and dropped the hand into the drawer.

"I'm not here for you, John Martin. You're just the audience. This time..."

It laughed again. Cleo's cell phone rang, and it ran out of the apartment.

Something else stayed.

"I AM here for you, John Martin."

The voice was cold.

Like ice cracking under you feet.

It chilled the whole room.

The light started fading away...

64

The back of my head hit something hard.

"Detective Martin!"

The cold, dark fog evaporated. The IA investigator stared into my eyes. I glanced at her nametag.

Johnson.

I blinked.

"Nice of you to join us, Captain Martin!"

Did I mention that I hated sarcasm?

"Detective Johnson," I took a big breath and let it out. It was hard standing up, but I wasn't going to let some sarcastic, blonde, big bobbed bitch…

"Nice to meet you."

"Lay off him, Claretta."

Claretta?

Johnson backed away.

My head hurt.

Lisa glared at me from behind Claretta 'Chesty' Johnson.

Damn.

"I thought I'd told you not unless I was here…" Lisa was pissed.

"Doc, I, uh, it was my little sister, Lisa. I had to."

Po is very good at begging forgiveness.

Lisa shined a light in my eyes.

"You okay?"

"You're the doctor."

Crack.

My cheek stung.

"Ow! What the hell was that for!"

Crack!

Lisa slapped me and turned in an easy motion, then walked out of Po's apartment.

Damn.

5

Nothing happened for a week.

Lisa had let me back into our apartment. I think Po lobbied her for a couple days, then demanded she get me out of his place.

She didn't say much.

I wanted to tell her I'm sorry, but I wasn't sure what I was sorry about.

And I'd probably say something to make things worse.

So I didn't say much either.

Nothing happened with the case, except that Mac got more pissed each day.

Po didn't leave Cleo alone much, except when she had to rehearse. She wouldn't let him stay for that.

I covered for him with Mac as best I could, but I don't think she bought it. Then again, she never called me on it either.

Friday night came. Cleo's show.

Po insisted we be there.

We sat in the front row. Cleo sang her hits, and a few new numbers. The crowd went nuts.

Then the fire alarm went off.

There wasn't any smoke.

Folks managed an orderly exit. I went out to check them in case they came back in. After about twenty minutes I lost Lisa in the crowd. I was looking for her over the top when somebody yelled that the door was locked.

It took me ten minutes to get inside.

Those thirty minutes outside the club changed everything.

Two uniforms had been at the front door, two more at the stage door. I told the two out front to keep the crowd out as I went in.

Po was tied to a chair, tears running down his face.

What was left of Cleo was tied to a chair on stage.

Parts of her were scattered in the lake of blood on the stage floor. Parts of her were missing.

"Where the hell were you?"

I flipped my pocketknife and cut Po free.

That was a mistake.

I saw a huge fist coming at me.

When I woke up two days later, Lisa told me what happened. I didn't remember anything.

It had somehow drugged Cleo and Po, tied them up, and woke them up. Po watched the thing cut up his little sister. One piece at a time.

That monster was steaming inside him, and this time it burst out.

I happened to catch the shrapnel.

I had six broken ribs, a few broken bones in my face, a concussion, and a broken arm. That took Po about ten seconds.

He took off after the thing in black, but there was no trail to follow. The two uniforms swore no one came out the stage door. Same for the two in front.

I was out of work for five weeks.

Mac came to see me once. She said Po went to work for the FBI, that I'd be getting a new partner when I got back.

Internal Affairs came to talk to me.
Chesty Johnson got a vicious squint from
Lisa when she asked her to step out for
the interview.

"What happened?"

"I have no idea. Po was upset. Who
wouldn't be if they'd been through that.
I was the first thing in range. After
that, I don't remember."

"Po said he thought you were the
thing that did that to Cleo. I tried to
tell him, that monster was too short to
be you. He's just…"

"Yeah. I know."

Johnson looked at me, a tear rolling
down her cheek, "He's in therapy. I made
him go. He blames you, John. Stay away
from him."

"He's my best friend. I can't. If
he's hurting, I should…"

"No, you shouldn't. John, he blames
you. You should have been there to stop
it. You should have seen it coming.
John, leave him alone. Let us go to the
FBI and forget about Po."

"Us? As in…"

"Yeah. As soon as it was an investigation of Po hurting you, I had to get off of the case. Po and I are… I've resigned, and took that FBI gig. I talked them into taking Po, too. Mac gave him a glowing reference. It ended her problem quietly.

"We had to keep us a secret, or I'd be off IA."

Po had a girlfriend and I didn't know about it?

"Damn."

Johnson left. Lisa came in.

"How'd it go?"

"I lost my best friend."

"He almost killed you John."

"That wasn't him. He was in shock, mad…"

"And you get beat up for it? John, he's…"

"Drop it. He's not a bad person. I've known him too long. That wasn't him."

"Who was it, the boogeyman?"

"He's your friend too."

Lisa stared at the floor for a long time.

"John, I don't know if I can…"

"What?" It came out sharper than I
wanted.

"I can't worry that you'll survive
the day, every day!" She ran out of the
room.

Damn.

Funny how you think about a lot of
things when you've got nothing else to
do.

Funny how the pain meds make you
forget most of it.

I spent a few weeks at home. Lisa was
there, taking care of me, when she
wasn't at work. She pushed me harder
than the physical therapist did during
my rehab.

I think she enjoyed it.

I kept waiting for Po to stop by. I
had it all planned out, how he'd say he
was sorry and I'd tell him not to worry
about it.

That never happened.

And that hurt more than his fists
had.

The morning I was going back to work
she came home about an hour before I had
to leave.

"John, I talked to Po last night."

I just stared at her for ten minutes.

It was five seconds.

"And?"

"He's the same Po. Except sad. John, he still blames you."

"Do you blame me?"

"John, you know better than that."

"Do I?" My monster got a foot out the door and shoved it open. Wide. "I fight off a pass from Cleo, and you trust me so much that you act like I'd taken her to bed. Now all of a sudden, you're chatting up the guy who tried to kill me, and then you tell me that you don't want me to be a cop? What am I supposed to do, back flips?"

She just turned and walked out.

Damn.

I don't really blame Po. But if he still blames me…

Po can be stubborn.

I know him too well. His monster came at me through his fists.

Mine came out and cold-cocked Lisa with my words.

Someday maybe I'll learn to keep my damn mouth shut.

I walked into the precinct ten minutes late. Mac was next to the door tapping her foot.

"My office, now, Martin."

Damn.

I followed MacDonald to her office. She moved around behind her desk, "Shut the door."

I did.

That's when I saw her.

Five feet ten inches of feminine perfection.

Perfect face. Perfect hair. Perfect lips. Perfect figure.

"Hello, Detective Martin."

Perfect voice.

I sat down quick.

I had to.

"John, this is Detective Patricia Margaret Theresa O'Rourke. Your new partner."

DAMN!

"Ah, er, hi."

Smooth. Real smooth.

"Orient her to the precinct. Shadow
Williams and Reichert this afternoon.
Oh, and John, you're on thin ice. You've
been out too much lately. That's all."

"What about the…"

"You're off of that case. Schuster
and Garfunkel have it. Now, get to
work."

I looked at my new partner.

My new, perfect partner.

"C'mon, O'Rourke."

"You can call me Patty."

Patty. Wagon.

Don't go there.

"Then come on, Patty," I held the
door of Mac's office open and motioned
her to go through it.

She walked perfectly.

Like she had heels on.

She didn't.

DAMN!

I could feel the precinct's
background noise cut out as Patty walked
across the room.

At least three pencils hit the floor.

"There, the messy desk. You sit on
that side."

I really didn't need this. I'd been with Po so long I couldn't remember the orientation policy.

Fortunately my phone rang.

"Martin."

"Detective Martin, this is Steve Walter from WNBC. I'd like to interview you about the Cleopatra case."

Damn.

"Sorry, you'll have to go through channels."

I slammed the phone down.

"Is everything all right, Detective Martin?"

Perfect. Her voice was perfect.

"Lord, why me?" I looked at the ceiling.

"You'll never be tasked with more than you can handle, John Martin."

"Yeah. Well." I suddenly realized I was staring at her chest.

"Um, Patty?"

"Yes, Detective Martin?"

"Your badge."

"My… Oh. OH! Where should I put it?"

"Inside jacket pocket. You're a detective, not a uniform."

"Yes, Detective Martin."

This was going to be a long day.

I brought Patty over to meet Williams and Reichert.

"Chris, Jeff, this is detective Patty O'Rourke, my new partner. Mac says we should shadow you two today."

I waited.

Patty stood there, hand extended.

Chris and Jeff sat there, mouths open like a saloon on payday.

"Eh-HEM! Chris, Jeff, this is Detective Patty O'Rourke, my new partner."

"Pleased to meet you, detectives!"

Perfect.

I thought they would melt into their chairs.

"Williams! Reichert!" Mac can be very loud when she's pissed.

Did I mention that Mac is pissed most of the time?

"Eh, Nice to meet you, ma'am!"

"Miss."

Great.

"Pleased to meet you, Patty." Jeff seemed a little in control. Chris was still staring.

The phone woke him up.

"Williams. Yeah. Where? Got it." Chris had never taken his eyes off of Patty.

"Some one broke into the All Angels Church at 80th and Broadway. Two homeless guys are dead on the alter."

"We'll follow you." I turned to Patty.

"You should drive, Detective Martin."

Good enough. I figured driving would take my mind off of a lot of things.

"You're married," Patty pointed at my ring.

"I think so."

"You are troubled, Detective Martin."

"Yeah, you could say that."

"I just did."

"Oh, Lord!"

"He is listening, Detective Martin."

What did Mac hang on me here? I had to change the subject.

"Call me John."

Worst thing I ever did.

"Yes, John. You are troubled by a falling out with your wife. And by your previous partner. It will all work out. Have faith."

Damn.

I managed to stay close to Williams, even though he drove like Richard Petty on speed. I pulled the Crown Vic in next to Williams' Lincoln Town Car.

I got out. Patty was waiting by the Crown Vic's front fender. We headed into the church behind Williams and Reichert, Patty a half step behind me.

"God have Mercy!"

It came as a whispered plea from behind me.

"Damn."

"John Martin!"

"Sorry."

"And…"

"Forgive me Father."

Jeff walked around the two bodies. Chris scanned the church.

As I got closer, the M.E. stood up.

Damn.

If Lisa's eyes had been shotguns, Patty would have been blown in half.

"Lisa, I thought you were…"

"I'm doing overtime."

Ice.

"Lisa, this is my new partner, Patty O'Rourke. Patty, this is my wife, Lisa."

"Yeah. Hands off. He's mine."

DAMN!

"I, eh, I'm pleased to meet you, Mrs. Martin."

Lisa stared at Patty's hand for ten seconds.

She turned to Reichert, "Stabbed. About a dozen times each. This one's missing his right hand. Looks like a serrated blade." She turned back to me, "Don't. Please."

"I wasn't thinking of it."

"Good." Lisa let out a big breath, "I'm sorry. We'll talk tonight?"

"Me too. Yes. I'll bring the pizza."

Lisa leaned in and kissed my cheek and whispered, "I'll have the Scotch on ice."

She smelled like jasmine.

I smiled.

"Nice to meet you Patty," Lisa growled before walking off.

Williams and Reichert were staring at me.

"What?"

They just shook their heads.

We all went to work.

Williams found some bloody footprints. Reichert found a bloody handprint.

Patty found the knife.

I pretty much just watched.

You get into a routine when you have a partner for a long time. You split up the workload, so to speak.

I felt like a rookie without Po.

"John, what do you think of this?" Patty pointed to a devotional candle, knocked over but not burning.

"It was put out before the struggle."

I was back in detective mode.

Between the four of us, we had a good idea of what happened. Williams and Reichert took off to look for any leads at the soup kitchen around the corner. Patty and I went to lunch.

I was thinking Mac wasn't punishing me at all. She was easing me back into things.

We stopped at Allessandros. I bought Patty lunch. Feeling useful was worth the $12.75.

I was thinking about Lisa putting the Scotch on ice…

Priceless.

I'd almost bitten into my gyro when my cell went off.

MacDonald.

Damn.

"Martin."

"Get your butts back here, now."

She hung up before I could ask why.

Not good.

"Wrap these please, Gladys? Patty, we have to go."

"Okay. You drive."

Damn.

I really wanted to eat that gyro.

I had half of it shoved into my mouth as we walked into the precinct. Mac glared daggers at me, but waited until I'd swallowed.

"You two have a new assignment. The President is at a financial district hotel. Half of his Secret Service detail is stuck in traffic, their car broke

down. The other half is lost in midtown.
I need you two to get there and secure
the President's limo until they can get
to it."

I raised an eyebrow at Mac.

"NOW!"

"I need an address."

"320 Pearl Street."

"John, you drive."

I was beginning to see a pattern
here.

It seems the Secret Service didn't
have a breakdown at all. The
Philanderer-in-Chief had lost them so he
could meet some bimbo at the hotel.

He wanted us to get her out without
either of them being seen.

Then he saw Patty.

He stared, mouth open like a rummy in
a distillery.

Then his instincts kicked in.

"Well, Detective! How would you like
to see the inside of Air Force One?" he
took a step toward Patty.

Before I could cut him off, Patty
stepped in front of me.

"Mr. President, you are a married man! What would your wife think? What would your constituency think? What would your mother think? Most importantly, what would God think of you making a pass at me after you've spent the afternoon in a hotel room with a woman of 'ill repute'?"

The word 'repute' was punctuated by a loud slapping sound as Patty's hand hit the President's cheek that coincided with the arrival of the Secret Service agents.

Damn!

Patty turned to the black suits and batted her eyes.

Three of them froze.

One wasn't impressed, and moved forward.

I stepped between them. My badge stopped him.

Well, his face ran into my badge.

Okay, his face ran into my fist that was holding my badge.

Okay, maybe my fist holding my badge moved a bit.

Fine, I slugged the guy, okay?

Hey, she's my partner.

The second reached for his firearm.

"Now, agent," I swear the Glock was melting, "you really don't want to explain how you lost the President for two hours," Patty leaned in close. Somehow, the top two buttons on her shirt had come undone, "Do you now?" Her finger traced a line down his cheek.

Patty turned and walked away.

The four agents and the President watched her walk.

I watched for five seconds before I followed her.

We'd just sat in the car when my cell went off. I tossed it to Patty as I headed down Peck's Slip. I didn't want to be there when those Secret Service agents realized what just happened.

"O'Rourke. Yes, Detective Williams. I'm fine, how sweet of you to ask. Yes. Okay, Chris. Now, really… No, I don't think that would be… Hello, Detective Reichert. I see. We'll be there as soon as possible. Thank you."

Patty slid the phone into my jacket pocket.

I caught a whiff of her scent.

Perfect.

But, it wasn't jasmine.

"Well?"

"Detective Williams asked me something. I said no. Detective Reichert said they've found parts of the church victims. It seems to be a pattern, like…"

"Like bread crumbs," I hit the steering wheel hard.

"Damn!"

"John Martin!"

"Sorry."

"What else?"

"Forgive me Father."

"Drive to 12th and Broadway. Williams and Reichert will meet us there."

This was becoming a long day.

We got there just as Lisa did. Four uniforms were keeping the crowd back.

"Detectives, this lady found… Wow!" Kawalski stared at Patty.

Tires screeched as traffic stopped.

I was noticing a pattern here.

"Kawalski, snap out of it. What happened?"

"Uh… Sorry, Detective. This lady here found this hand here on this here corner." Kawalski pointed to an empty space to his right, his eyes still glued to Patty.

"What lady?"

Kawalski spun around in a circle, "The lady, she was right here…"

"Did you get a name, officer?"

"I, um, not yet. I told her not to go anywhere… Damn it!"

"Officer!" Patty frowned at Kawalski.

"Oh, sorry, Detective." Kawalski crossed himself, "Forgive me Father."

"Okay, what did she look like?"

"Forty-ish, well dressed. Silver hair, big rings…"

Patty took the description from Kawalski while I got statements from the ones in the crowd who had seen her.

Everyone said the hand just appeared.

I looked over Lisa's shoulder.

Yup, it was a hand.

I think.

Hard to be sure without any fingers on it.

Williams and Reichert got there just as I asked Lisa, "Is that a hand?"

"Yes. A right hand."

Damn.

I did a quick calculation in my head. The church was north of here, so…

I had the uniforms spread out towards the south.

It didn't take long to find the first finger.

Broadway and Amsterdam Avenue meet at 71st Street.

The index finger was there.

The thumb was at Broadway and 8th. Columbus Circle.

The pinkie was found at 50th and First.

The ring finger showed up in Cavalry Cemetery, just off of Gale and Greenpoint.

The 'finger' was found in Our Lady of Mount Carmel Cemetery, near Woodhaven and 66th.

Back at the precinct Patty was sticking pins in the Big Map.

It looked like a spiral. Pointing to Belmont.

We all stared at it for 45 minutes.
Then we shrugged and went home.
Lisa had the ice and the Scotch.
I forgot the pizza.
It didn't matter.
We never did get to the Scotch.
She knew exactly how to…

6

I looked down at her sleeping in the crook of my arm. Happy. Gorgeous.

I couldn't sleep.

Every time I closed my eyes I saw fingers.

I'd been through this before. It took me twenty years to get over it.

Well, to bury it.

You don't get over seeing your kid brother chopped to pieces.

But when I looked at Lisa, everything was right in the world.

"Hmmmm… You are amazing!" Her eyes were open.

That voice… it just melted me.

Damn!

I forgot about fingers for a while. Again.

I ran my finger down her nose. I couldn't stop smiling.

"What's she like?"

Damn!

"Patty?"

"No, Mata Hari!" She slapped my chest.

"Ow! I don't know. She's…" This is usually where I shoved both feet into my mouth, as far as they would go, "She's, well, she's the prettiest woman I've ever seen, and smart too. She has guts. She's a good detective. Traffic stops for her…"

Lisa had turned away from me.

"Do you…"

"I can partner with her. Sure."

Wrong answer.

Damn.

I couldn't sleep next to the iceberg Lisa turned into. I went looking for the rest of the Scotch.

I found it.

Lisa woke me up by slamming the door on her way to work. Right after my cell rang with Patty's call.

It took me a few minutes to splash some water on my face, run a razor over it, grab a clean shirt and suit, and make my way to the Crown Vic.

Patty was waiting by the right front fender.

I drove to the precinct, pretty much in a haze. About halfway there Patty woke me up.

"You should look. You would see something."

Yeah, good thing Lisa didn't hear that.

We were sitting at a light, so I looked at her.

She was looking straight ahead. She was almost glowing.

"It could help catch the killer before another victim dies."

I took a big breath, then let it out.

I'd sort of promised myself that I would never do that again. I connected it with Po's rage.

I knew Patty was right.

But…

"How did you know?"

"A little Angel told me."

The blaring horn behind woke me up.

Patty stared straight ahead.

No glow.

For a while I wasn't sure if I'd dreamt that conversation or not. I figured it must be the Scotch.

"We should stop at Mount Carmel."

Damn!

"John Martin!"

How did she hear me think that?

"Forgive me Father."

I drove to the cemetery.

The gravesite was marked by yellow police tape. We ducked under it and moved to the white circle.

There was no wall around, so I lay down next to the spot where the finger was found.

It wore a long black gown, black lace veils flowing in the breeze. It bent over and placed the finger next to me. As it bent, it turned towards me.

I could see into the hood, past the veils.

Into nothing.

Deep, dark, nothing.

Suddenly I was cold, frozen almost. I couldn't move but to shiver. It bent over me, the nothingness coming closer, inches from me. The hood was like a giant mouth, ready to swallow me. A sleeve reached out to touch me.

I tried to scream.

It didn't work.

The world seemed to shrink away from me, spiraling into a tiny pinpoint of light, but it stayed near me, reaching for me…

I felt her lips on mine.

Her hand on my cheek.

Her voice, tender and comforting in my ear…

"John. Come to me, John."

My eyes opened. I saw her eyes, the love there.

"Lisa. I am so glad to see…"

Crack!

Lisa's pretty strong for a Doctor.

My cheek hurt.

I was beginning to see a pattern here.

"Hey, what?"

She was walking away. Fast.

Damn.

I stood up and looked for Patty. She was sitting nearby, rubbing her jaw.

Damn!

"Did you see anything?"

"Yeah. Death."

Patty shot up to her feet, looking very concerned.

"Did it… touch you?"

"No. Almost, but no."

"We must leave this place," Patty sighed heavily. "Our answers are no longer here. Next time, we need to get there sooner."

Next time?

"What makes you think I want to do that again?"

"You don't want to, John Martin, but you will. Because you want to solve this case."

My cell went off. I grabbed it.

MacDonald.

"Yeah." I was drained, and I sounded like it.

"You awake, Martin? Get in here. Williams and Reichert are on their way in for a briefing from Central." Click.

That's what I like about Mac. Always willing to hear your side.

I managed to stumble towards the Crown Vic, weaving a tortured path through the headstones. I was just about to ask Patty to drive…

"John Martin, you drive."

I don't remember the trip, other than Patty mumbled a lot. It sounded like prayers.

I fell into my chair. A few seconds later Patty set down a large coffee in front of me.

"Thanks."

I took a test sip.

Perfect.

I downed about half of it.

The guy from Central droned on about tight lips and publicity inciting panic or something like that. He said there was some plan to investigate this with a team approach, a few detectives here and there working on individual leads.

Sounded like a load of crap to me.

I was just about to say that when Patty chimed in her perfect voice, "What a unique approach!"

I let it go with a sigh. If the big paychecks want to mess this up, well, we'll still take the fall. But we'll all know whose fault it is.

When everything broke up, Mac walked over to me. She just stared for ten seconds, then leaned down.

"This is a load, but we need to live with it. Do what you can under their parameters," Mac straightened up. "You look like he…" she shot a look at Patty's frown, "Take the afternoon off. O'Rourke has to take her marksmanship tests."

I'm sure I mumbled something. Maybe. Next thing I knew I was home in bed and someone was beating on the door.

I sat up and yelled, "Just a damn minute!" followed reflexively by, "Forgive me Father." I sat up and reached for my robe.

The note was there.

I knew the handwriting. I had an idea of what it said.

I grabbed the robe and cracked the door.

"Yeah?"

"Detective Martin? It's Steve Walter from WNBC. May I have a few minutes?"

Between the hangover, the near brush with Death, and what I knew was in Lisa's note, I was numb.

"Sure. C'mon in."

That's when I saw the empty Scotch bottle and the sofa cushions on the floor. The kitchen was half covered in whipped cream…

"Pardon the mess."

"No prob…lem, de…tec…tive."

"What's your angle?"

"I'm just looking for information, Detective Martin. What can you tell me about the Hansel and Gretel murderer?"

Great. It has a name.

That was never good.

Me talking to reporters was never good, either.

I just didn't remember that right now.

"Central has some cockeyed scheme to have detectives track individual leads. It's a crock. They'll never solve this case that way. They need to find a lady dressed in black, looks like Death…"

Did I just say that?

Damn!

"John?"

That perfect voice rang from the open door. Walter stopped his frantic scribbling to stare with his mouth open.

"Patty? How was…"

"My scores? 50 out of 50."

Perfect.

Figures.

Did I mention I saw a pattern here?

"Eh, um, excuse me, miss…"

"Detective O'Rourke," I waved my hand between them, "Walker, reporter."

"Pleased. Mr. Walker, the detective is not well. He's on sick time. Please…" Can eyelashes really bat that fast? Patty had the poor guy heading for the door, "Let him get his rest. Thank you now. So long." Patty shut the door behind him.

I don't think he even knew he was being ushered out.

"Really, John. You should clean up this place. Lisa would so appreciate it," Patty was tossing cushions back on the couch.

"Get moving, you slug!" Patty scooped up some whipped cream and flung it at me.

I flung it back.

Just as Lisa opened the door.

Damn!

I tried to go after her. She was gone.

I came back into the apartment, studying the carpet.

"John, I'm so sorry…"

"Just go, please. It's not your fault, it's mine."

Patty left. I opened the cupboard and pulled out the Scotch Lisa bought the other day.

I brought the bottle into the bedroom. Lisa's note was there, glaring at me.

"Dear John,"

DAMN!

"Dear John, I am so sorry. I love you so much that the thought of losing you is unbearable. Please forgive me. I'll make it up to you tonight, I promise.

"Yours forever, Lisa."

I took a swig of Scotch.

I never tasted it.

I thought about things. How every time my life seems really nice, something ruins it.

Usually something I say or do.

Or don't do.

Like holding my brother's hand tight enough that day at the airport…

Suddenly I was twelve again, watching Dad's plane taxi up. Feeling James' hand slip from mine.

Watching him run towards the plane.

Seeing the plane turn towards him.

Seeing him hit the propeller.

The numb feeling was drowning me again.

Or maybe it was the Scotch.

I know when I woke up, it was a shock.

Mac was staring at me.

"I was wondering if you'd ever wake up. O'Rourke is worried sick about you. The M.E.'s office called, Taylor is worried sick about Lisa. I figured you'd be in rough shape, but this… Really, John."

"I…" I tried to sit up.

It didn't work.

My ribs still hurt.

My head pounded.

"Where's Lisa?"

"She's with a friend."

I knew who. Maybe it was a good thing for all of us. Maybe not.

It's not that I didn't trust Lisa. Or Po.

Life had just beaten me too numb to think about it.

"Here. Coffee. Drink."

Mac, a nursemaid? Go figure.

"John, I need you back. O'Rourke is good, but she's a rookie. Williams is adequate, but on this case he's clueless. Reichert is competent. You're the best detective I've ever seen.

"Central is reeling. They're all over my ass on this. It seems some one blabbed their investigation plan all over the news."

DAMN!

"Look, Mac, I…"

"I had to do a lot of fast talking to Central to cover your ass, Martin. I called in a few favors, too. The only thing that will save all our asses is to solve this thing fast."

Good ol' MacDonald. Pissed off as usual.

I started to feel a little more… normal.

I gulped the coffee and stood up.

Bad move.

Sometime after Patty left I had stripped down.

"Really, Martin! Put some… Eh-hem. I'll just, um, wait out there…"

I think Mac was blushing.

I grinned.

Back to work.

Mac drove me to the precinct. The first half of the trip was silent.

"Can you 'see' this one?"

"I tried. I'm not sure what I'm seeing though. Mostly it's like a bad dream. Nightmare, really.

"Hey, Mac, how did you get in to my place, anyway?"

"You left the door open."

"Great. Monsters chasing me and I can't even lock the friggin' door."

We got on the elevator. I hit the button.

I caught Mac glancing down *there* out of the corner of my eye.

It was all I could do not to laugh out loud.

The doors opened and the same old Mac was barking orders to the precinct.

I felt better.

Patty gave me a smile.

"You all right?"

"No, but I'll manage. Let's get a move on. Williams, Reichert, c'mon. I want to see those sites on the map."

"These are in green. Ignore the blue ones. They're from…"

"Yeah." I swallowed Staten Island.

Somehow I pushed Cleo and Po out of my mind and only saw the green pins.

"They curve down and around… out this way. It looks too much like a pattern to be random…"

"Yeah, right. Don't let anyone near it. We'll be there as soon as we can," Patty hung up the phone. "They found another finger. Grumman Road East."

"Bethpage?"

Damn.

"You drive."

We made it there in 45 minutes.
Pretty good time.

The finger was on a bend in the road,
near the old Grumman Aircraft factory.

I shot a glance at the place.

"Thank God it's not there anymore."

I didn't know I'd said that out loud.

"John?"

"Grumman Bethpage Airfield. His
brother died at an airfield." I turned
back to see Lisa looking at a dark spot
on the ground.

Patty gasped and looked at me.

"This finger's not from those
homeless guys in the church. It's been
here too long." Lisa dropped the finger
into a bag and stood up, still looking
down. "I'm taking it to the lab. I'll
let you know if I find anything."

She walked away without looking up.

Halfway to her van she stopped.

"John, promise me. You won't."

She hadn't turned around.

"If I have to, I have to."

She walked the rest of the way to her van.

"Lisa, wait! I…"

The van drove off.

"John, you're thinking something."

Yeah.

That my life just drove away.

"I've got a hunch this is tied to something else. Lisa will tell me if I'm right."

We looked through, around and under the bushes and trees. We combed the parking lot.

Nothing.

We drove back to the precinct. I wanted to check something out.

I went straight to the map.

I stuck a pin into Grumman Bethpage Airfield.

I stepped back and looked at all the pins.

"Damn!"

"John Martin!"

"Forgive me, Father."

"Holy crap!" Williams said from over my shoulder.

"Christopher Williams!"

"Forgive me, Father. I'll be da…
would you look at that."

The pins lined up.

All the pins.

The pins from the Excelsior Club. The
pins from Cleo. The pins from the
homeless guys.

They all pointed to Grumman Bethpage.

MacDonald walked up to the map. She
grabbed a half dozen white pins and
stuck them into the map.

She stepped back.

A line of six white pins made a
straight line from Bethpage to the
precinct.

"Bethpage. Hofstra. Queens. Hunters
Point. Sutton Place. The Precinct. The
five places I have lived and the place
where I work."

We all stared at Mac.

"I have no idea if it means anything.
Find out."

She went into her office and closed
the blinds.

We stared at Mac's office for a
while. Reichert finally broke the
trance.

"Anyone want some coffee?"

"I'll go with you," Williams and Reichert slinked toward the elevator.

I walked towards Mac's office.

"John, what are you going to say?"

"If I'm not out by sundown, call a priest."

I went in and closed the door behind me.

"What?" Mac lifted her head up from the desk. She didn't look good.

"What's eating you?"

"What do you think?"

"I think you're twisted up over the thought that you could be the cause of all this crap."

"You're a good detective." Her head went down again.

"Bullshit."

Mac lifted her head, "No, you really are."

"That's not what I meant. You can't blame yourself for this. We don't even know for sure if you're connected to this."

"Yeah. Right." Her head went back down.

"DAMN IT Mac! The precinct needs you. Get your shit together."

"If I wasn't here…"

"This would be happening anyway. This is Evil, Mac. The kind of Evil we're here to stop. We need you riding our asses to keep our minds from turning inside out over this. We need you now. On top, coordinating, pushing us to think from a new angle."

"No shit?" She sat up and cocked her head.

"No shit."

Mac took a big breath and let it out slowly.

Her eyes squinted at me.

"Then what the hell are you doing in here, Martin? Get to work!"

I couldn't help grinning a bit as I turned and walked to the door. My hand hit the knob…

"And Martin, don't you ever come in here without knocking again."

I did my best to wipe the smile off of my face before Patty saw it.

Her smile was… perfect.

Mac came out and marched to the elevator.

"I'll be back in twenty minutes. Don't go anywhere."

Williams and Reichert came back with four coffees just ahead of Mac. She looked at the coffees and squinted at Williams.

"Thanks for remembering that I don't drink coffee," Patty smiled.

Mac dropped a pile of books on my desk, grabbed a coffee and pulled a chair over.

"Well, what are you waiting for? These are my yearbooks and photo albums. We need to go over these to see if there's a connection. Let's get to work."

We poured over the yearbooks and photo albums. Mac would describe a boy here, a girl there.

We were getting nowhere and taking a long time to do it.

Just before nine Lisa came in. She had two pizzas and six coffees.

"I figured you'd be hungry." She moved some papers on Reichert's desk and set the food down. She lifted her head slowly and looked at me. "Take a break and get something to eat."

I could breathe again.

Lisa looked like she was embarrassed for a second. Then she took a big breath.

"The Bethpage finger is from the first girl."

Damn.

Lisa looked at the library of Mac's life on my desk, "What's this?"

"The locations of the… parts all point to Bethpage. I was born in Bethpage, went to Hofstra for Criminal Justice Administration, and lived here, here, and here. We are here right now. It can't be a coincidence."

"Hmm. Any ideas?"

"We've been over all my rivals, old boyfriends, friends. Nothing."

"He wouldn't be so obvious in your life. He'd be in the background, desperately craving your attention, but not doing anything overt to get it. He would be very subtle."

We all looked at Lisa.

"What? I have a PhD in Criminal Psychology."

"We aren't sure it's a 'he'. I couldn't tell, and the build was kind of small."

"Oh, it is a 'he'. A skinny little mousey 'he' in the background shadows of your life."

"Did you minor in poetry too?"

"Funny, Jeff. But that's where you'll find him. In the shadows," she picked up a yearbook and began flipping through it.

The rest of us were busy with the pizza and coffee.

"I thought you didn't drink coffee, O'Rourke."

"I didn't until just now."

"Right." Mac leaned close to Patty's ear.

Yeah, I listened.

She's my partner.

"This precinct depends upon teamwork. You're a perfect fit."

Patty took a gulp of coffee.

Three hours later we called it quits. We weren't any closer to a break, and

Mac thought we'd do better after some sleep.

Lisa and I watched Patty, Reichert, and Williams leave.

"Go home you two." Mac commanded as her office light went out.

"She won't leave until we do."

"Good boss."

"Yeah."

"Lisa," Mac stood in her office doorway, arms folded, foot tapping, "John needs a ride home."

We didn't say anything on the ride.

I was afraid I'd say something stupid.

When Lisa parked her car, I froze.

I didn't know if she'd come home or not.

"John, are you planning on sleeping in the car?"

She was waiting by the front fender.

I got out and walked to her. I found her hand and held it as we walked up the stairs.

We didn't say much when we got to the apartment. We were both exhausted.

I said, "I'm sorry."

She said, "I'm sorry."

We went to sleep.

I didn't sleep well.

Oh, I held Lisa. She still fit into that comfortable spot on my shoulder.

But every time I dozed off…

Death came.

Like a frail old lady shrouded in a cloak of black woven from nothing.

Walking slowly toward me.

Each time I fell asleep, it was closer.

The fourth time it reached out, almost touching me…

"JOHN!"

I sat up, Lisa clinging to me.

"I have to see it again."

My head throbbed from lack of sleep, too much coffee, and yesterday's Scotch.

"Why?" Lisa held me tighter, "Why?"

"I saw something. Something that could tell me where to look."

I felt Lisa's lips kiss my forehead, her fingers stroke my head…

It was looking at me, hooded head cocked to the left.

"John Martin, you should not be here."

It reached out for me, but stopped short. It seemed puzzled.

I looked past it. There, a glimmer in the distance, a ruffle of cloth…

A stage.

A play.

A boy, a girl.

Breadcrumbs.

Hansel and Gretel.

The actors, maybe ten years old.

"Yes, the same age as James…

"Aaargh!"

"John!"

My head spun, I couldn't focus.

"John, look at me."

Lisa, caressing my face, bringing me back.

Slowly.

Calmly.

I turned to look into her eyes.

"Hansel. It's Hansel."

I got to the precinct just before Mac did.

I always thought she slept there.

I was looking through her grade school yearbook.

Nothing about a play.

"Martin, you're early."

"Mac, what do you remember about the play, 'Hansel and Gretel'?"

Mac's eyebrows shot up.

Williams walked in grinning.

Behind Patty.

"Fifth grade play. I played Gretel." Mac's eyebrows dropped about twelve floors, "Why?"

"Who played Hansel?"

"Heh. I don't remember his name. He was a quiet guy, never talked to anyone. They gave him the part out of pity or to try and get him to open up, or both. He never said the lines out loud in rehearsal, he'd just whisper them to Mrs. Hart." Her face darkened a bit,

"During the play, he forgot his lines. I had to whisper them to him. I got mad. I remember telling him…"

Mac fell into Patty's chair.

Reichert walked in. It was still too early for anyone else.

"Do you think… I told him he shouldn't be on a stage ever. All this because I yelled at the kid for forgetting his lines? Good grief Martin."

"Show me his picture."

"I can't. He never came back to school. The class pictures were taken after he left."

"What did he look like?"

"That was a long time ago."

We got an artist in. Mac gave her best recollection. As the face took shape, her memory got better.

After two hours we had a sketch of the perp at ten years old.

Great.

"Does the name 'Igor Katella' sound right?" Patty pointed at her computer screen, "He transferred to Plainview

Elementary in early December of his fifth grade."

Mac looked over Patty's shoulder.

"DMV puts his address as 31st Street and 21st Ave."

"That's him. Good work, O'Rourke. Print the DMV pic. Williams, Reichert, bring him in here. It's early, so he should be home."

"Mac, Patty and I…"

"Williams and Reichert."

I slumped back into my chair.

"Martin, you and O'Rourke hit the crime scenes again," Mac stood and looked down at me, "Look around. Tell me what you see."

Damn.

"You drive," Patty said as she walked toward the elevator.

Yeah, a pattern. No doubt about it.

The underground nightclub never reopened. Patty called the building's super to open it up.

We turned to face the sound of footsteps.

"Lisa?"

"Mac called, said I should be here," she shook her head, "Insisted. She made it sound like your health was involved," Lisa glanced at Patty and frowned.

"Mac wants me to…"

"Damn."

Patty started to say something, but Lisa cut her off.

"I don't like this, John."

"I have to. It's the only way we can be sure. I need to be sure."

The super walked to the door, mumbling obscenities.

"Mr. Carvel!" Patty wasn't going to be denied a second time.

The super looked at Patty. His expression… humbled is the only word I can come up with.

"Forgive me, Father. Here you go. Don't wreck the place."

"Stay outside please. We'll be less than a half hour."

"Gladly. This place gives me the willies. The lights are on the wall to the left."

Patty hit the switch as we went in.

Lisa grabbed my arm and shivered, "The blood stains are still here."

I swallowed Long Island.

"Let's get this over with."

"John," Patty stepped next to Lisa, "You are never tasked with more than you can handle. And you will never be forsaken."

"Let's hope you're right."

I ran my fingers lightly over the bloodstain. I'd expected it to be sticky. It wasn't.

But it still smelled like iron filings.

I sat on the stain and lay back. I spread my arms out along the floor and took a deep breath.

I could hear Patty as I closed my eyes, "…Valley of the Shadow of Death, I will fear no Evil. Thou art with me. Thy rod and Thy staff they comfort me…"

What was left of the girl was tied to the chair. It walked around the chair in circles, looking from the chair to the audience.

It spread its arms and opened its mouth…

I saw the face. Pale. Scarred. Frowning.

I saw the Adam's Apple.

Most likely male. Five-five, maybe 160.

It was trying to speak, but nothing came out.

It stomped around the stage in anger.

It gathered the body parts and left.

I followed it into the alley. When it tossed the ski mask into the dumpster, I saw the face…

It was Igor Katella.

When he turned the corner at the end of the alley, something… stepped out of him.

Something dark. Hooded.

By a cloak woven of nothing.

Death walked towars me, its pace quickening as it drew near…

"I have those around you. Then I will come for you. How long can an hour be? A lifetime?"

"John…" Her hand on my cheek…

"You do what is Right, so come to his rescue…"

Death faded into a receding pinpoint, collapsing into the nothing it came from.

I looked at Lisa, then Patty.

"It's Igor. Mac, we have to get to Mac. I'll drive."

Lisa and Patty both reached for the front passenger door.

"We don't have time. Just get in!"

"John, you've got to clean back here!" Lisa glared from the backseat.

I stopped the Crown Vic in front of the parking garage elevator. I glanced at my watch.

12 minutes since…

The sign on the elevator door said "OUT OF SERVICE."

Damn.

I ran up the stairs. I stopped at the precinct's stairwell door to catch my breath.

I hate running.

I heard Patty and Lisa about two floors behind me as I opened the door.

The entire precinct was out cold.

I gasped, and the room started spinning.

122

Lisa pulled me into the stairwell.

"Smells like an anesthetic. An aerosolized form is used for large animals, like cows and horses. We need to wake them up as soon as possible, before they asphyxiate. Head for the windows."

Lisa grabbed my shirt and ripped it into three pieces.

"Cover your mouth and nose. The cloth should stop the droplets from getting into your lungs." She folded her fabric three times and pressed it over her mouth and nose.

"They'll still have one hel…" Lisa glanced at Patty, "a bad headache when they wake up. Let's go!"

It only took a few seconds to open the windows. Lisa went to each detective and uniform, checking pulses, slapping them to stimulate their breathing.

"How do we know it's safe to breathe in here?" Even through four layers of cotton cloth Patty's voice was perfect.

"They'll start to wake up."

123

Williams woke up first. Within a few seconds, everyone was awake. I checked my watch.

22 minutes.

"Where's MacDonald?"

"I don't know. We walked the suspect into her office. The next thing I remember…"

I didn't wait for him to finish.

I was down the stairs and in the Crown Vic before Lisa and Patty could follow.

I didn't have time to wait for them.

I knew where he was taking Mac.

I scraped a fender on the way out of the parking garage.

I was on the radio as I hit the lights and siren.

"Get everyone you can to Central Boulevard Elementary in Bethpage. The auditorium."

School was in session.

Igor would have his audience.

And Mac would be the star.

I made it in 18 minutes. That made it 40.

My hand hurt from pounding the
steering wheel.

The school doors were locked.

Three kicks and they were open.

Where's the Auditorium?

Next to the stairwell an evacuation
route was posted.

I glanced at my watch as I sprinted
down the hallway.

48 minutes.

I drew my gun and kicked the
auditorium doors.

They seemed to open in slow motion.

About a hundred kids were crying,
tied to the seats.

Igor was on the stage, next to the
chair Mac was tied to. He had a knife in
one hand, about six inches from Mac's
right hand.

The Colt 45 makes a very loud noise
when it's fired.

I didn't hear it.

I could see the bullet moving out of
the muzzle flash.

It took forever to travel the 200 or
so feet.

Igor's head exploded.

I watched the knife tumble out of his hand, like an autumn leaf falling down…

The clang of it hitting the stage floor brought everything back to normal.

"Police." I pulled my badge out and flashed it at the kids as I ran to the stage.

I picked up Igor's knife to cut Mac loose.

She just looked at me. When she was free she stood up.

"Martin, where in Hell is your partner?"

Epilogue

By the time the others got there, Mac and I had most of the kids free.

Williams got there first. Patty rode with him.

Lisa rode with Reichert.

Smart guys.

No matter what Mac says.

I.A. talked to Mac and me.

And the kids.

Somehow the little detail of me firing my gun outside my jurisdiction was resolved.

I gave Steve Walters an exclusive, with one condition.

Walters called Igor the 'Hansel and Gretel killer.' He kept his word.

He never mentioned Mac and the perp going to school together.

Lisa and I had some rough times over the next two weeks. Some of it was me working with Patty. Most of it was due to me talking faster than I think.

We were divorced three weeks after I shot Igor.

It was tough, being a homicide detective and having your ex-wife as the Medical Examiner.

We eventually got back together.

But that's another story.

I hope you enjoyed my story. If you did, please leave a review.

About James W. McAllister

I am a Registered Respiratory Therapist living near Syracuse in Central New York State. Currently I am employed in Healthcare Accreditation. I founded Fortiter Publishing LLC in November 2013 as a vehicle to get all these great Science Fiction and Fantasy stories out of my head.

"FORTITER" is inscribed on the MacAlister Clan Crest. The word means "to go forward, boldly." I am grateful for the Clan Chief's permission to use the Crest and Tartan in my company's logo, and to use "FORTITER" in my company's name.

I have been interested in science fiction since reading the Lensmen Series of books by E. E. "Doc" Smith in Junior High School. TV shows like Star Trek and Battlestar Galactica, and movies such as Robinson Crusoe on Mars and Star Wars further peaked my interest in the genre.

Other books by James W. McAllister

RODS
Another John Martin Story

STARCLAN Book I
THE TURRET
Starclan Foundation

STARCLAN Book II
THE BEST LAID PLANS
Birth of the Starclan

STARCLAN Book III
A MATTER OF HONOR
Starclan Chrysalis 2016

THE PAGE
The Year of the Dragons

THE UNIVERSE,
While You Wait
28 short stories to read
while you're waiting

See my Amazon Author's page here:
http://amazon.com/author/jwmcallister